This book is a work of fiction. Any references to historical events, real people, or real places are used fictitiously. Other names, characters, places, and events are products of the author's imagination, and any resemblance to actual events or places or persons, living or dead, is entirely coincidental.

LITTLE SIMON
An imprint of Simon & Schuster Children's Publishing Division • 1230 Avenue of the Americas, New York, New York 10020 • First Little Simon hardcover edition March 2020 •
Series designed by Laura Roode.
Book designed by Hannah Frece. The text of this book was set in Usherwood.
Manufactured in the United States of America 0120 FFG 10 9 8 7 6 5 4 3 2 1
Cataloging-in-Publication Data is available for this title from the Library of Congress.
ISBN 978-1-5344-6019-5 (hc)
ISBN 978-1-5344-6018-8 (pbk)
ISBN 978-1-5344-6020-1 (eBook)

ures of

MOUSE

16

Hattie in the Spotlight

By Poppy Green • Illustrated by Jennifer A. Bell

LITTLE SIMON
New York London Toronto Sydney New Delhi

Contents

Chapter 1:
Hattie Hides from the Spotlight
1

Chapter 2:
A Surprise from Mrs. Wise
11

Chapter 3:
Sophie Says the Wrong Line
21

Chapter 4:
Hattie's Hidden Talents
37

Chapter 5:
Team Hattie!
51

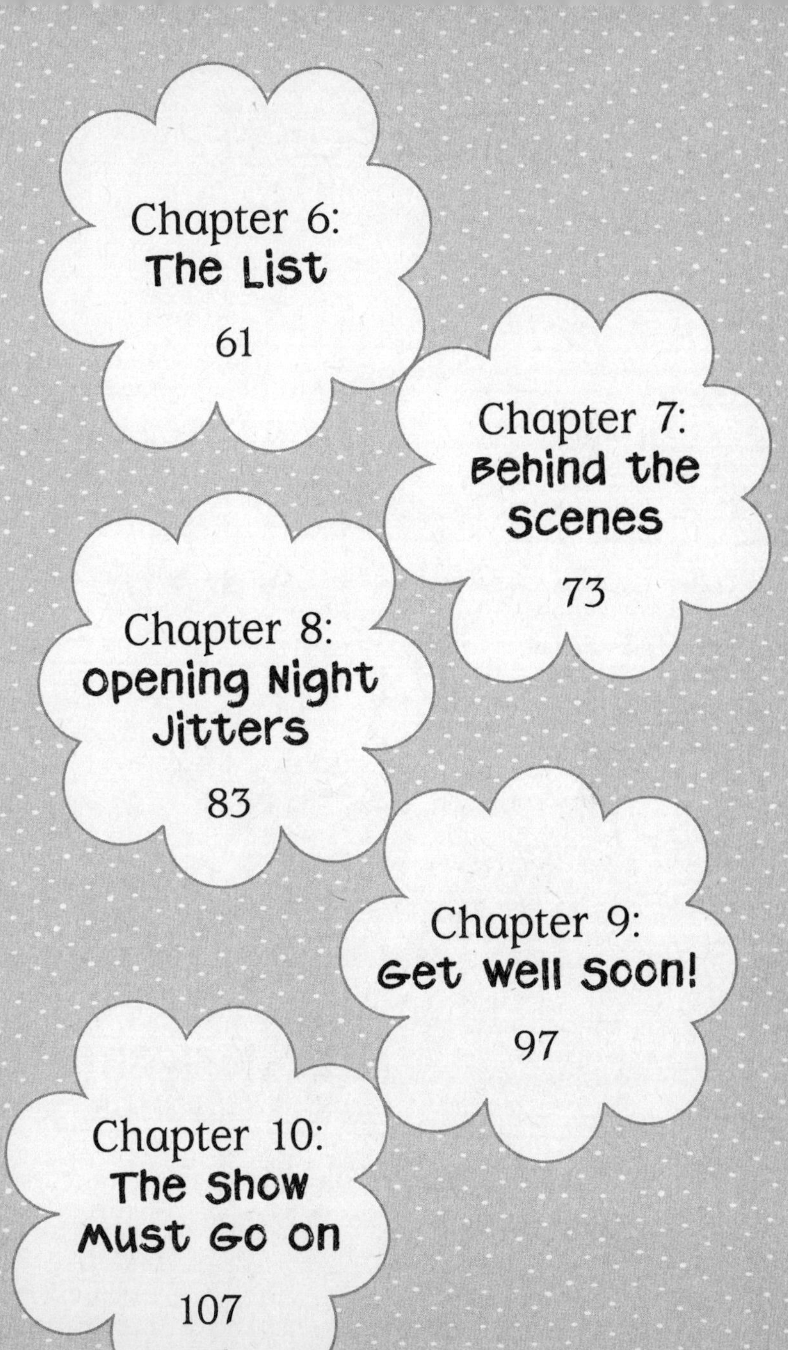

Chapter 6:
The List
61

Chapter 7:
Behind the Scenes
73

Chapter 8:
Opening Night Jitters
83

Chapter 9:
Get Well Soon!
97

Chapter 10:
The Show Must Go On
107

— chapter 1 —

Hattie Hides from the Spotlight

Sophie closed her eyes and stretched out on her raft.

The springtime sun was warm on her face. Her friends Hattie and Owen swam nearby, talking and laughing. The water lapped gently at the sides of the raft. All was peaceful on Forget-Me-Not Lake until—

Splash! Owen and Hattie splashed her from the water.

"Ah!" Sophie sat up and opened her eyes. She used her oar to splash Owen and Hattie back. "Water fight!"

Hattie ducked under the water. Like most frogs, she was an excellent swimmer. She resurfaced on the

other side of the raft. Hattie splashed Sophie from that side. Owen splashed Sophie from the other.

"No fair!" Sophie called out. "Two against one!"

Owen used his long snake tail to splash Hattie. She dove underwater again.

"Where did she go?" Owen said.

He and Sophie scanned the water's surface.

Sophie heard a rustle in the reeds behind her. She whirled around, expecting to find Hattie. "Ah-*ha*!"

Instead, Sophie was staring down at two young ducks.

"Wah!" one of them quacked in surprise.

"Sorry!" the other duck said. "We weren't trying to spy on you. It just . . . looked like fun."

Sophie laughed. "That's okay!"

"Want to play?" Owen asked the ducks.

"Sure!" the first duck said eagerly. Her eyes focused on something over Sophie's shoulder. "But are you sure your friend doesn't mind?"

"Huh?" said Sophie. She turned around.

Behind some rocks, Sophie could make out a green nose and one eye. It peeked out at them through flower-rimmed eyeglasses.

"So *that's* where Hattie went!" Sophie cried. She leaned close to the ducks and whispered, "She's a little shy. But only at first." Then Sophie had an idea.

Sophie organized them in a game of leapfrog—Hattie's favorite. The more they played, the farther Hattie came out into the open.

"Hattie!" Sophie called out. "We could use one more to make our leapfrog line longer!"

Hattie hesitated for a moment. Then she smiled and leaped over to join in. Before long, Hattie was laughing loudest of all.

"They were nice," Hattie said later about the ducks.

She and Sophie and Owen were on the path back to Pine Needle Grove. Close to town, they came around a bend. Sophie could make out the brand-new roof of Oak Hollow

Theater up ahead in the distance.

"Have either of you been inside the theater?" Owen asked.

Hattie shook her head.

"Not since they reopened," Sophie said.

Ever since they could remember, Oak Hollow Theater had been a rustic outdoor theater: log benches arranged on a slope in front of a simple stage.

But recently it had been redone. The Pine Needle Grove Arts Council had hired a great architect for the project—Sophie's dad, George Mouse! A huge group of volunteers had raised the new roof and decorated the inside.

Sophie had seen the plans on her dad's drafting table. But not the real thing. "Should we take a peek?" Sophie asked. Owen and Hattie nodded.

As they pushed open the front doors, Sophie could not believe her eyes.

chapter 2

A Surprise from Mrs. Wise

Instead of benches, now there were real seats for everyone. With seat cushions. And armrests.

There was a brand-new balcony.

The stage had a plush red curtain that opened and closed.

Sophie pointed up at the ceiling. "Look!" she cried. It was painted a midnight blue with tiny gold stars.

"It's just like a night sky!"

"And with a roof, no shows will be rained out," Owen said.

"It's so beautiful," Hattie said, marveling at the theater. "I can't wait to see a play here. I wonder when the first show will be."

On their way out the door, Hattie found her answer.

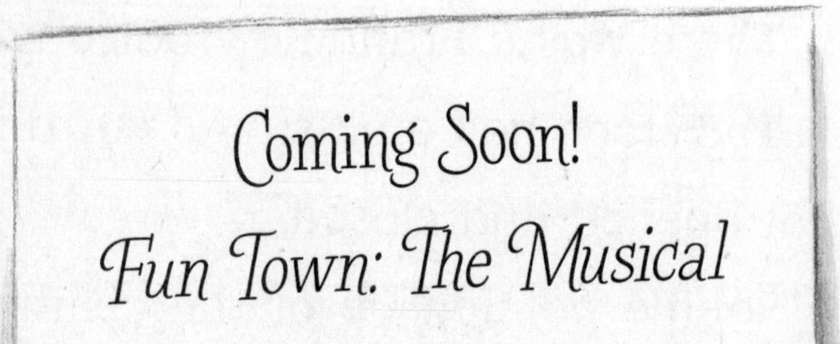

Coming Soon!

Fun Town: The Musical

Presented by

Pine Needle Grove Arts Council

That night, the Mouse family sat down to a dinner of potato pie.

"Dad, the new theater is amazing!" Sophie raved.

Her little brother, Winston, pouted. "I haven't seen it," he complained.

Sophie described the inside. Then she told them about the poster she had seen. "Can we get tickets to see *Fun Town*?" she asked.

Mrs. Mouse nodded. "Yes! I heard about that," she replied. "Mrs. Wise is the director."

Sophie and her brother, Winston, looked at each other in surprise. Mrs. Wise was their teacher at Silverlake Elementary.

"I don't know if you know this," Mrs. Mouse continued. "But Mrs. Wise is an excellent musician. Before she was a teacher, she conducted a large choir."

Mr. Mouse passed around the chive biscuits. "I believe she also plays the flute quite well."

At school the next morning, Sophie slid into her seat. At the front of the classroom, Mrs. Wise had her back turned. She was writing on the board.

Sophie gazed out the window. Mrs. Wise . . . an excellent musician?

Sophie daydreamed a scene of Mrs. Wise at home. She was playing a difficult classical piece on her flute. It was almost as if Mrs. Wise had a different life outside school!

"Class!" Mrs. Wise's voice rang out. The students quieted down. "Before morning math, I have an announcement."

Sophie snapped out of her daydream. She saw what Mrs. Wise had written on the board.

Oh! Sophie sat up straight. She wanted to hear this.

"Coming soon to the *new* Oak Hollow Theater," Mrs. Wise said, "is a wonderful play called *Fun Town.*"

Sophie looked over at Hattie and Owen. They nodded knowingly at one another.

"As the play director," Mrs. Wise went on, "I would like to invite you all to audition to be in it!"

Wait. What? thought Sophie. *Be in it?*

"It's about the mayor of a town that used to be a

wonderful place to live, but has fallen on hard times," Mrs. Wise explained. "Lots of animals have been leaving. So the mayor has to find a way to attract visitors—*and* convince the animals who are there to stay."

Mrs. Wise said she was looking for actors of all ages. She held up a sign-up sheet for auditions. Then she smiled.

"Maybe the next star of the stage is . . . you," Mrs. Wise said.

chapter 3

Sophie Says the Wrong Line

The playground was abuzz about the play. All through morning recess, Piper the hummingbird flitted from classmate to classmate.

"Are you going to audition?" she asked Sophie.

Sophie thought it over. "I don't know," she replied. "Mostly I want to go see it!"

Piper turned to Owen. "You?"

Owen shook his head no. "I'm not great at memorizing lines," Owen explained.

“Hattie?” Piper said. “Are you interested?”

Hattie opened her mouth as if to speak. But she seemed unsure of what to say.

“Oh, Hattie hates the spotlight,” Sophie told Piper. “She wouldn’t want to audition.”

Sophie looked at Hattie and smiled. She expected Hattie to smile back in agreement.

Instead Hattie’s cheeks blushed a bright red. She looked down at the ground.

Then Hattie turned and slowly walked away.

Sophie felt a knot tighten in her stomach. Hattie was upset. And Sophie was pretty sure it was her fault. She hurried after her friend.

Hattie walked to the edge of the playground. She sat down under some ferns.

Sophie sat next to her.

"Did I say something wrong?" Sophie asked.

Hattie picked a leaf up off the ground. She twirled it in her fingers. “It’s just . . . I had an idea,” said Hattie. “I guess it was a bad idea.”

Hattie kept her eyes locked on the leaf in her hand.

“What was it?” Sophie asked gently.

Hattie shrugged. She took a deep breath.

"I *was* thinking about auditioning," Hattie said. "For the play. Maybe." She looked up at Sophie now. "But you're right. It doesn't seem like me, does it?"

Sophie put a hand on Hattie's shoulder.

"Oh, Hattie, I'm so sorry," Sophie said. "When you didn't answer Piper right away, I thought it was your way of saying no. But I shouldn't have answered for you. I think you would be *great* in the play. You should audition. You really should!"

Hattie frowned. “I don’t even know what I’d have to do,” she said uncertainly. “I’ve never auditioned before. For anything!”

Sophie's whiskers twitched. "Well, let's go ask Mrs. Wise!" she suggested. "She'll tell you."

Sophie stood up. Hattie hesitated.

"If you want, I'll help you get ready for your audition!" Sophie promised. "I could help you learn lines or song lyrics. Like an audition coach!"

A slow smile spread across Hattie's face. "Okay," Hattie said, getting up. "Let's go."

"Hooray!" Sophie cheered. This was going to be even better than trying out herself.

— chapter 4 —

Hattie's Hidden Talents

"I'm very pleased you're auditioning, Hattie," Mrs. Wise said.

She wrote Hattie's name on the sign-up sheet. It was official! Auditions were in five days. Hattie would need to learn one of the songs from the play. And she needed to memorize a few lines from a scene of her choice. Hattie even got a copy of the script!

After school, Sophie and Owen followed her all the way home, reading over her shoulder.

Sophie scanned the list of roles.

"Oooh. Franny, the mayor's daughter!" Sophie read out loud. "It says she has lots of spirit and lots of opinions. That sounds like a good part!"

"Or Sarah?" Owen read out. "Editor of the school newspaper."

There were parts that were clearly for grown-ups, like Ma Ferris and Old Mister Stevens. But there were many young-sounding parts, too.

"Which role would you want to play?" Sophie asked Hattie.

"I don't know," said Hattie. "There are a lot of characters." She flipped through a few more pages. She came to a song page. The melody was written out in musical notation. "Hmm, I wonder how this song goes."

They had arrived at Hattie's house. When they got inside, Hattie took the page over to her mom's piano. She set it on the music stand and began to plunk at the keys.

Owen rushed over. "You can read music?" he said in surprise.

Hattie nodded.

Sophie knew Hattie took piano lessons. But she'd never heard Hattie play!

Then Hattie cleared her throat and began to sing the words. She sang quietly at first.

"Welcome, welcome to our town.

"Come right in and sit right down . . . ."

Hattie's voice slid easily from one note to the next. With each line she got a little more confident. Her voice grew louder.

"We want our town to make you smile.

"So you'll decide to stay a whiiiiiiiiile!"

The last note was long and high. As Hattie held it, it became a powerful, dramatic croak.

When she stopped, Sophie and Owen clapped enthusiastically.

"Hattie!" cried Sophie. "Your voice! It's amazing!"

Hattie's eyes went wide. "It is?" she said.

"Yes!" Owen replied. "Why don't you sing more often?"

Hattie beamed. "I don't know," she said. "I didn't think anyone wanted to hear it."

Sophie put an arm around Hattie's shoulders. "Folks are going to want to hear it," she assured her.

Owen nodded in agreement. "Hattie, I hope you are ready to be in the spotlight."

— chapter 5 —

Team Hattie!

As Hattie's audition coach, one of Sophie's tasks was to make sure she rehearsed every day.

The next day, Tuesday, they read through some lines. Sophie read the part of the mayor. Hattie was Franny, his daughter. Owen was the audience.

"Very convincing!" Owen said. "I really believed it. Hattie, you're good at pretending to be rude."

"Aw. Thanks, Owen!" Hattie replied.

On Wednesday, they went over a funny scene. Hattie practiced speaking loudly and clearly. "If they can't hear you, they won't get the joke," Sophie pointed out.

And on Thursday and Friday, they focused on music. Hattie had to choose a song to sing at the audition. She liked "Good Morning, Main Street." It was the first musical number of the show—fast, catchy, and high-energy. They worked on a few easy moves Hattie could do to the music.

“This feels a little silly,” said Hattie as she did jazz hands. “How does it look?”

“It looks like you’re having fun!” Owen replied.

“Are you having fun?” Sophie asked her.

Hattie couldn’t help smiling. “I am,” she said. “I really am!”

Sophie gave a thumbs up. “Then I think you’re ready!”

Saturday was the big day. Sophie had promised Hattie that she would meet her at the theater before her audition.

But Sophie was running late! She hurried along the path to Oak Hollow Theater.

When she got there, the front doors were closed. A few animals with scripts milled around outside. It looked like they were waiting for their audition times.

Hattie was nowhere to be seen.

Sophie walked up to the theater doors. She stood on tiptoe and peeked in through the window.

There was Hattie—onstage!

Sophie was too late to wish her luck. But she looked like she didn't need it!

Hattie was standing in the spotlight. She was singing. She was smiling. She was doing jazz hands!

Sophie stepped away from the door. She sat down on a rock to wait. Then she jumped up again. She paced back and forth. She just couldn't *wait* to talk to Hattie and hear how it went.

The theater doors opened.

Sophie jumped. "Hattie!"

But it wasn't Hattie. It was Mr. Handy from Handy's Hardware, and a rabbit Sophie didn't know.

They walked off, deep in conversation.

"We've seen some great auditions today," the rabbit was saying.

Sophie's ears pricked up. Maybe they were talking about Hattie.

"Yes, indeed," replied Mr. Handy. "But the play won't be anything if we don't have a good set."

A set? thought Sophie. Like scenery and backdrops? Like *designing* and *painting*? These were two of Sophie's favorite activities. She wanted to hear more.

But just then, the doors opened again. Out stepped Hattie. She looked triumphant.

Before Sophie could ask, Hattie gave her the report.

“I don't know how well I did,” Hattie said. “But I did it!”

chapter 6

The List

That night, Sophie lay awake in bed. She imagined her bedroom ceiling was a blank canvas. On it, she pretend-painted backdrops for the stage of *Fun Town*.

One was a storefront. Another was a school. Maybe there could also be a library—and a bakery! The backdrop of Town Hall could have real wooden steps in front of it.

Sophie was eager to get back to the theater on Sunday morning. The cast list was going to be posted on the door. She wanted to be there when Hattie found out which part she got.

Because Sophie was *sure* she'd gotten a part.

The three friends had agreed to meet in town after breakfast. When Sophie got there, Hattie looked nervous.

"Don't worry," Sophie told her. "I have a good feeling about this."

Together they headed off to the theater.

LIBRARY

Sophie walked briskly. Owen kept up. But Hattie kept falling behind. She was walking so slowly! Twice Sophie and Owen stopped to wait for her.

"Don't you want to find out?" Sophie asked her.

Hattie kicked at a pebble. "I'm not sure," she replied glumly.

A group of animals was crowded around the theater entrance. They were squinting to read a paper tacked to the door.

Sophie and Owen held back. "You go ahead," Sophie told Hattie. "We'll be right here."

Hattie stepped slowly forward. Patiently, she inched her way to the front of the crowd.

Sophie watched Hattie as she scanned the cast list. Starting at the top, her finger moved down, down, down the paper. Surely, any second now, Hattie would find her name.

Wouldn't she?

Hattie was still reading. She was almost at the bottom of the list. For the first time, Sophie felt a pang of doubt. What if—?

Then Hattie's finger stopped moving. She turned to look at Sophie and Owen. Her face lit up with a brilliant smile. She came rushing over to her friends.

"Franny!" Hattie cried gleefully. "I'm going to be Franny, the mayor's daughter!"

The three friends jumped up and down, clinging to one another. “That’s a big part!” Sophie exclaimed.

Owen cheered. “Congratulations, Hattie!”

— chapter 7 —

Behind the Scenes

Hattie hurried home to tell her family the big news.

Owen headed back to town. He needed to get a few things for his mom at the General Store.

But Sophie had a question she needed to get answered.

She pushed open the theater door and peeked inside. Not far away,

Mr. Handy was talking with Mrs. Wise. Then Mrs. Wise hurried off backstage.

This was Sophie's chance! "Excuse me, Mr. Handy?" she said, hurrying over. "I heard you might be looking for help with the set?"

Mr. Handy took off his hat. He scratched his head as he looked down at Sophie.

"Sophie Mouse?" Mr. Handy replied. "Are you saying *you'd* be interested?" He sounded skeptical—as if he wasn't convinced Sophie was up to the job.

Sophie almost turned around and left.

Instead she took a deep breath and answered confidently. "Yes. I would."

Mr. Handy was silent and still. When he suddenly spoke, Sophie jumped in alarm.

"Wonderful!" Mr. Handy boomed. "That's just splendid. We can use all the help we can get!"

"Can you come to rehearsal tomorrow?" Mr. Handy asked. "You can get started. And we'll find you some helpers. The set designer needs helpers."

Sophie nodded. She couldn't wait! "I'll be there!"

The next few weeks were a blur of school, homework, and play rehearsals. Every free moment was filled with *Fun Town*.

Owen signed up to help with lighting for the show. So now all three friends were in the cast or crew. On the one hand, they *saw* one another every day. On the other hand, they didn't spend much time together because they were so busy preparing for the show.

They each had different jobs.

Owen was learning how to aim the spotlights and run the lighting board. There were switches and dials for each light. They could go on or off, bright or dim, and even change color.

Sophie made sketches of sets and backdrops. She worked with Mrs. Weaver, the seamstress, to make huge fabric canvases. Then Sophie directed the painters. They transferred her designs onto the canvas. The backdrops were hung from the stage rafters and dropped down for different scenes. Sophie also worked with Mr. Handy. They made movable wooden set pieces—like the Town Hall steps.

And Hattie was constantly onstage. At first, Mrs. Wise and the actors practiced one scene at a time. They ran through lines. They decided who would stand where. They learned dance moves.

And as the weeks went on, they ran through the whole play over and over again.

In the role of Franny, Hattie had two big musical numbers: “Get Out While You Can” and “A New Day.” Her voice was perfect for them.

Backstage, at work on the sets, Sophie smiled whenever she heard Hattie singing. Hattie sang the songs so many times, Sophie had them memorized too.

— chapter 8 —

Opening-Night Jitters

"Okay, everyone," Mrs. Wise called out. "That's a wrap!"

The final dress rehearsal was over. The entire cast and crew of *Fun Town* gathered on the stage.

"Tomorrow is opening night," Mrs. Wise said. "Everyone get a good night's sleep. Rest your bodies and your voices."

Sophie, Hattie, and Owen walked out of the theater together.

Sophie sighed with relief. Her work was done. The sets were in place. The stage crew knew all the cues. They would take care of changing the scenery during the shows.

"I can't wait to watch from the audience tomorrow!" Sophie exclaimed.

Hattie let out a deep breath. "I sort of wish *I* could watch from the audience."

Sophie and Owen looked at her curiously. "Are you nervous?" Owen asked.

Hattie nodded. "What if I forget my lines?" she said. "What if I freeze onstage?"

She covered her face. "What if I'm not meant for the spotlight?"

Sophie gave her a squeeze. “Trust me,” she began, “Owen and I have seen you onstage all these weeks. You are amazing up there!”

They walked Hattie home. On the way, they reminded her how well she knew her part.

"I bet you could say your lines in your sleep," Owen said.

Hattie laughed. "Probably," she agreed.

"And your songs," said Sophie, "you've sung them literally a hundred times. I haven't heard you mess up once."

“But I’ve never done it in front of a big audience,” Hattie pointed out.

They had arrived at Hattie’s front door.

"Just remember this," Sophie said. "The audience is going to be full of family and friends. The friendliest audience you can imagine. And all rooting for you!"

Hattie nodded. Then she said good night to her friends. "Thanks," Hattie said before closing the door. "I feel better."

Early the next morning, Sophie was in the kitchen eating her oats and berries. "Only twelve hours until the show!" she said to Winston next to her.

Suddenly there was a loud knock at the front door. Sophie went to answer it. She swung the door open. There stood Hattie. Her eyes were wide in alarm.

"Aw, Hattie," Sophie said, "don't worry! We told you last night. You're going to be fine—" Sophie stopped.

Hattie was shaking her head urgently. She pointed at her own throat. "Sophie," Hattie whispered.

"What is it?" Sophie asked. "Why are you whispering?"

"Because," Hattie whispered back, "I lost my voice!"

"You lost your voice?" Sophie cried.

Hattie's panicked expression suddenly made perfect sense. Tonight was opening night. Hattie had a big role, but she had no voice!

"Uh-oh," said Sophie.

— chapter 9 —

Get Well Soon!

Sophie sprang into action. "It's okay," she told Hattie. "I'll meet you back at your house. And I'll bring help."

Then Sophie ran upstairs. She changed out of her pajamas and into her clothes. She ran down to the pantry and gathered supplies. During the winter, her mom had lost her own voice from a bad cold. Sophie remembered all the things

Mrs. Mouse had used to get better.

Sophie packed them all in a basket. She told her mom and dad where she was going. Then Sophie ran to get Owen. On the way to Hattie's, Sophie told him why Hattie needed their help.

Sophie and Owen found Hattie in the kitchen with her mom. Hattie opened her mouth to say something.

Sophie held up a hand. “No talking,” she said. “You need to rest your voice.”

Hattie nodded in silent agreement.

“Good advice,” Mrs. Frog said. “I’ll put water on for tea.”

“Great!” said Sophie. “I brought some slippery elm bark tea. My mom says it soothes the throat.”

Mrs. Frog made some and served

Hattie a cup. She sipped at it dutifully.

When Hattie's cup was empty, Sophie jumped up. "How about another?" She added some honey for extra throat-soothing power.

When Hattie couldn't drink another drop, they moved on to the next remedy.

"Steam!" Sophie declared. She filled a bowl with the leftover hot water. Hattie leaned over it and breathed in the rising steam. Sophie draped a towel over Hattie's bowed head. It created a tent over the steam bowl.

"Deep breaths," Sophie instructed.

Owen had the next idea. "My mom makes me nap when I'm not feeling well," he said.

So they sent Hattie off to sleep for a while.

When she woke up, Mrs. Frog gave Hattie a spoonful of elderberry syrup. "Seems to fix most things," Mrs. Frog said.

As the day went on, Hattie tried gargling with saltwater.

She drank a capful of apple-cider vinegar.

She wrapped warm scarves around her throat.

But eventually, their time ran out. Hattie had to start getting ready to go to the theater.

"Maybe you should test it?" Owen asked. "Your voice. To see if it's back?"

Hattie looked at her mom and Sophie. They nodded.

So Hattie opened her mouth. “Um . . . hello?” she said softly. It was rough. It was gravelly. But it was there.

The question was . . . would it last?

chapter 10

The Show Must Go On

Sophie fidgeted in her seat. She looked down the row of theater seats. Next to her, Winston looked sharp in his best shirt and tie. The whole Mouse family had dressed up for their night at the theater.

Oak Hollow Theater was packed. The play was about to begin. Sophie saw Owen take his seat at the lighting board behind the back row. He waved at her and raised his eyebrows, as if to say, *What's going to happen?*

Sophie tugged at her whiskers and shrugged. *I don't know!*

Then the house lights went down.

The musicians in the band pit began to play. The curtain went up.

And there it was: *Fun Town*, with sets designed by Sophie Mouse. There were the backdrops she had worked so hard on.

Around her, Sophie heard audience members gasp. There were even *oohs* and *aahs*.

Sophie grinned. They liked it!

The set *did* look magical. The soft lighting made it look like early morning in town. The lights sparkled off the bits of glitter Sophie had sprinkled on some of the scenery.

Actors made their entrances: the mayor and the shopkeepers. They delivered their lines, including a funny one.

The audience laughed! The opening number went off without a hitch.

It was going so well, Sophie almost forgot about Hattie. But then came the second scene—and Hattie's entrance.

Sophie knew exactly how it was supposed to go. She held her breath.

Hattie—or Franny—entered from stage right. She walked confidently across the stage. She stepped right up to her dad, the mayor. She stared him squarely in the face.

"No way!" Franny shouted. "I am *not* riding in a float in the town parade!"

Her voice was loud and forceful and clear as day. Sophie's heart soared. Hattie's voice was back!

Sophie sank back into her chair with relief. Now she could enjoy every moment of Hattie's performance.

Sophie craned her neck to see every time Hattie was onstage. She sang along with the musical numbers. She belly-laughed at Hattie's funny lines, even though she'd heard them all. She clapped and cheered loudly after Hattie's big songs.

Sophie was so happy for her—and so proud!

After the finale, the whole cast lined up onstage. The audience erupted into thunderous applause.

Sophie saw Hattie look around. When their eyes met, Hattie smiled a wide, proud smile. Then the cast joined hands and took a bow.

Sophie was the first one on her feet to give them a standing ovation.

The End

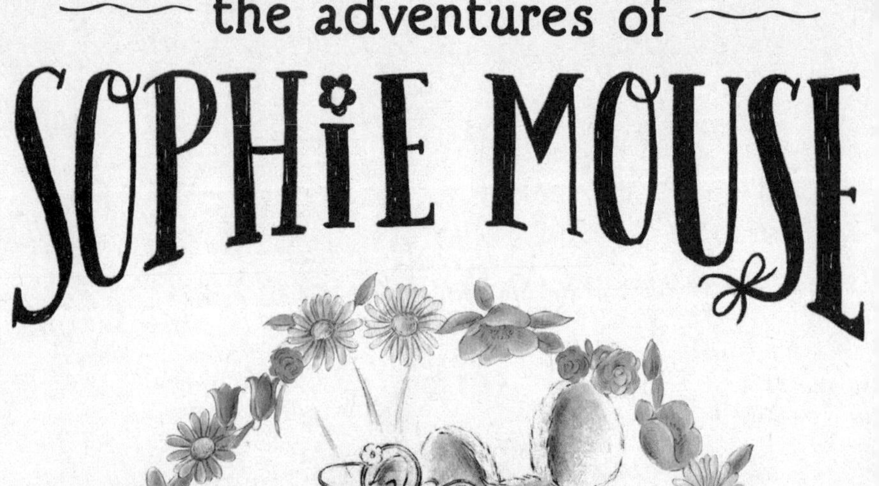

For excerpts, activities, and more about these adorable tales & tails, visit AdventuresofSophieMouse.com!

If you like Sophie Mouse, you'll love

the CRITTER club